FREDERICK WARNE

Published by the Penguin Group
Registered office: 80 Strand, London, WC2R ORL
Penguin Young Readers Group, 345 Hudson Street, New York, N.Y. 10014, USA

First published 1906 by Frederick Warne
This edition with new reproductions of Beatrix Potter's book illustrations first published 2007
This edition copyright © Frederick Warne & Co. 2007
New reproductions of Beatrix Potter's book illustrations copyright © Frederick Warne & Co. 2002
Original copyright in text and illustrations © Frederick Warne & Co., 1906

Manufactured in China

THE STORY OF
A FIERCE BAD RABBIT

BY BEATRIX POTTER

FREDERICK WARNE

THIS is a fierce bad rabbit;
look at his savage whiskers,
and his claws and his
turned-up tail.

THIS is a nice gentle Rabbit. His mother has given him a carrot.

THE bad Rabbit
would like some carrot.

HE doesn't say "Please."
He takes it!

AND he scratches the
good Rabbit very badly.

THE good Rabbit
creeps away, and hides
in a hole. It feels sad.

THIS is a man with a gun.

HE sees something sitting
on a bench. He thinks it is
a very funny bird!

HE comes creeping
up behind the trees.

AND then he shoots
— BANG!

21

THIS is what happens —

BUT this is all he finds
on the bench, when he
rushes up with his gun.

THE good Rabbit
peeps out of its hole,

AND it sees the bad
Rabbit tearing past
— without any tail
or whiskers!